DETROIT PUBLIC LIBRARY
3 5674 04852815 3
P9-EMH-114
SHERWOOD FOREST BRANCH
7117 W. SEVEN MILE RD.
DETROIT, MICHIGAN 48221
JUL 2008
SF

An ode to Poe for
Xian, Justin, and Kamaree

www.houghtonmifflinbooks.com

No crows were harmed in the making of this book.

The text of this book is set in Pabst.
The illustrations are collages of hand-dyed cut and torn paper.

Library of Congress Cataloging-in-Publication Data Number 2006026078

Printed in Singapore TWP 10 9 8 7 6 5 4 3 2 1

ISBN-13 978-0-618-66380-4

THE CROW

(A Not So Scary Story)

Alison Paul

Houghton Mifflin Company
Boston 2007

One morning I woke up sleepy,
came downstairs to something creepy.

Outside the window sat something freaky
my eyes had never known.

Quickly I crouched,
crawled and creeped

behind the couch,
where I could peek.

The floorboards creaked,
but he did not squeak,
or peep, or sing
outside my home.

Instead I peered to see him sitting,
this proud king
outside my home,
but it's my tree, not his throne.

So I slid myself along the floor
to this mystery I must explore.

closed the curtain even more,
so my face would not be shown.

I watched with a single eye,
through a crack where I could spy,
out at this ghastly guy,
this guy I had not known.

I caught him sneaking,
saw him leaping,
this slick robber on the roam.
Tiptoeing on the tip-tops
of the white picket fence
around my home.

There he floats,
filling me with fright,
for this wizard's not wearing white.

His cloak is black, deep as night,
casting shadows where he goes.

"CAW! CAW!" is the spell he calls,
telling darkness to crawl
along the walls
and down the hall,
making midnight fall on my autumn morn.

Now with a wave of his arms
he starts summoning stars
from past Pluto and Mars
and wrestles them onto his robe.

Could it be a crystal ball
that brought him to my home?

So am I watching him,
or is he watching *me?*
I feel I'm not alone.
As I pull the curtain back,
to make a bigger crack,
what is it I see?

His eye!
His big black eye on my eye.
His eye looking back at me.
This pirate peering through a spyglass,
out on the grass,
outside my home.
Seems he's stopped his ship,
to take a trip, into my home.
Does he want in?

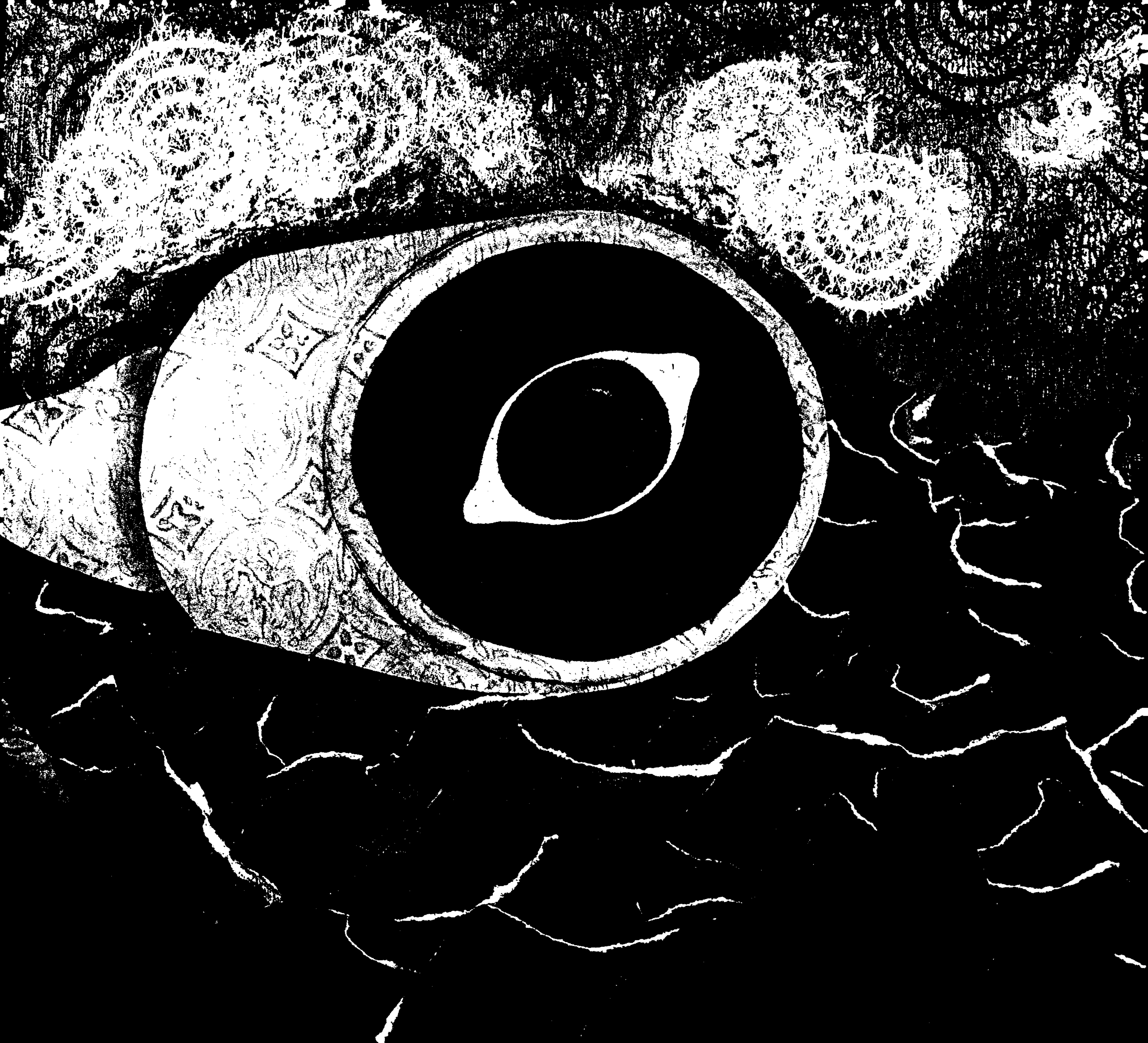

He won't be
shown in—
not into
my home.
No king
on a throne!
No thief
on tiptoe!
No wizard's
shadow!
No pirate's
rowboat!

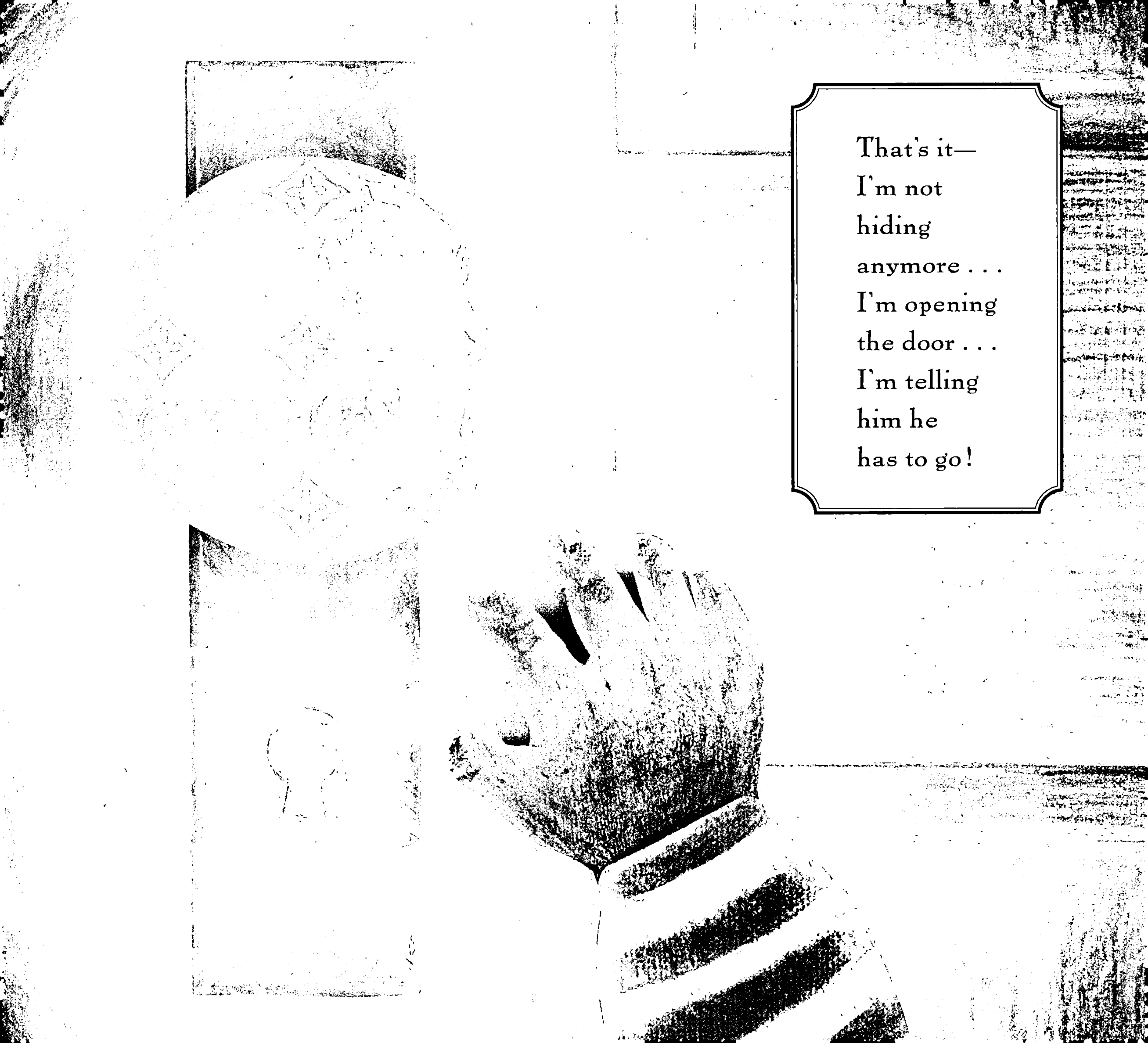

That's it—
I'm not
hiding
anymore . . .
I'm opening
the door . . .
I'm telling
him he
has to go!

Oh,

it's just a crow.

And now I see
that he was
just as scared as me.

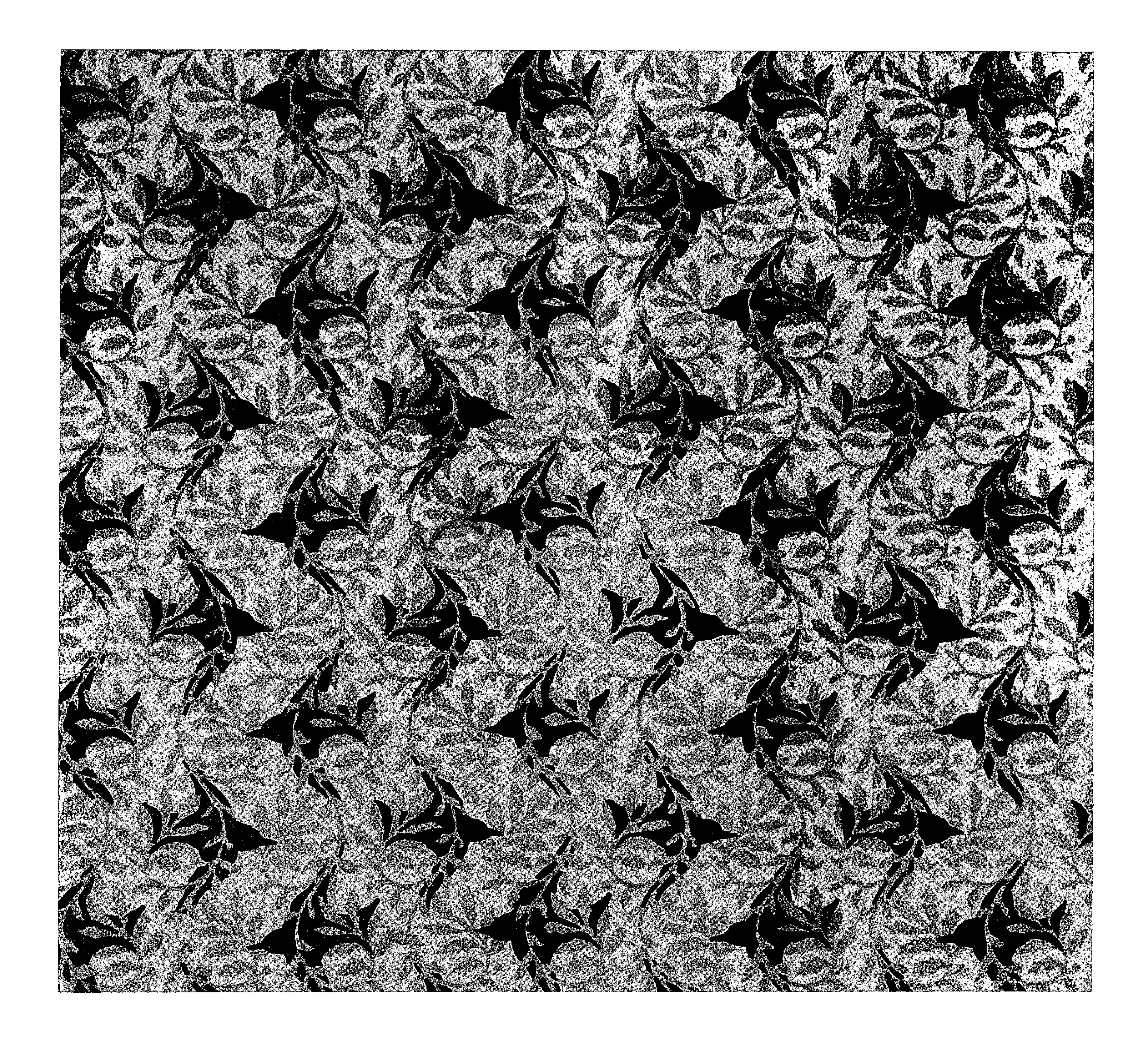